GW00862703

Stories taken from *The Helen Oxenbury Nursery Story Book*
first published 1985
This edition published 1995 by William Heinemann Ltd
an imprint of Reed Consumer Books Ltd
Michelin House, 81 Fulham Road, London SW3 6RB
and Auckland, Melbourne, Singapore and Toronto
Text compilation and illustrations
© Helen Oxenbury 1985, 1994, 1995

ISBN 0 434 974129

Printed in Italy

# HELEN OXENBURY

## Favourite Nursery Stories

## Contents

**HEINEMANN**

# The Little Red Hen

Once there was a pretty, neat little house.
Inside it lived a Cock, a Mouse and a Little
Red Hen.

On another hill, not far away, was a very
different little house. It had a door that
wouldn't shut, windows that were dirty
and broken, and the paint was peeling off.
In this house lived a bad old mother Fox

and her fierce young son.

One morning the mother Fox said, "On the hill over there you can see the house where the Cock, the Mouse and the Little Red Hen live. You and I haven't had very much to eat for a long time, and everyone in that house is very well fed and plump. They would make us a delicious dinner!"

The fierce young Fox was very hungry, so he got up at once and said, "I'll just find a sack. If you will get the big pot boiling, I'll go to that house on the hill and we'll have that Cock, that Mouse and that Little Red Hen for our dinner!"

Now on the very same morning the Little Red Hen got up early, as she always did, and went downstairs to get the breakfast. The Cock and the Mouse, who were lazy, did not come downstairs for some time.

"Who will get some sticks to light the fire?" asked the Little Red Hen.

"I won't," said the Cock.

"I won't," said the Mouse.

"Then I'll have to do it myself," said the Little Red Hen. So off she ran to get the sticks.

When she had the fire burning, she said, "Who will go and get the kettle filled with water from the spring?"

"I won't," said the Cock again.

"I won't," said the Mouse again.

"Then I'll have to do it myself," said the Little Red Hen and off she ran to fill the kettle.

While they were waiting for their breakfast, the Cock and the Mouse curled up in comfortable armchairs. Soon they were asleep again.

It was just at this time that the fierce

young Fox came up the hill with his sack and peeped in at the window. He stepped back and knocked loudly at the door.

"Who can that be?" said the Mouse, half opening his eyes.

"Go and find out, if you want to know," said the Cock crossly.

"Perhaps it's the postman," said the Mouse to himself. So, without waiting to ask who it was, he lifted the latch and opened the door.

In rushed the big fierce Fox!

"Cock-a-doodle-do!" screamed the Cock as he jumped onto the back of the armchair.

"Oh! Oh! Oh!" squeaked the Mouse as he tried to run up the chimney.

But the Fox only laughed. He grabbed the Mouse by the tail and popped him into the sack. Then he caught the Cock and pushed him in the sack too.

Just at that moment, in came the Little Red Hen, carrying the heavy kettle of water

from the spring. Before she knew what was happening, the Fox quickly snatched her up and put her into the sack with the others. Then he tied a string tightly around the opening. And, with the sack over his shoulder, he set off down the hill.

The Cock, the Mouse and the Little Red Hen were bumped together uncomfortably inside the sack.

The Cock said, "Oh, I wish I hadn't been so cross!"

And the Mouse said, "Oh, I wish I hadn't been so lazy!"

But the Little Red Hen said, "It's never too late to try again."

As the Fox trudged along with his heavy load, the sun grew very hot. Soon, he put the sack on the ground and sat down to rest. Before long he was fast asleep. Then, "Gr—umph . . . gr—umph," he began to snore. The noise was so loud that the Little Red Hen could hear him through the sack.

At once she took her scissors out of her
apron pocket and cut a neat hole in the
sack. Then out jumped: first the Mouse,
then the Cock, and last, the Little Red Hen.

"Quick! Quick!" she whispered. "Who
will come and help me get some stones?"

"I will," said the Cock.

"And I will," said the Mouse.

"Good," said the Little Red Hen.

Off they went together and each one
brought back as big a rock as he could carry
and put it into the sack. Then the Little Red

Hen, who had a needle and thread in her pocket too, sewed up the hole very neatly.

When she had finished, the Little Red Hen, the Cock and the Mouse ran off home as fast as they could go. Once inside, they bolted the door and then helped each other to get the best breakfast they had ever had!

After some time, the Fox woke up. He lifted the sack onto his back and went slowly up the hill to his house.

He called out, "Mother! Guess what I've got in my sack!"

"Is it – can it be – the Little Red Hen?"

"It is – and the Cock – and the Mouse as well. They're very plump and heavy so they'll make us a splendid dinner."

His mother had the water all ready, boiling furiously in a pot over the fire. The Fox undid the string and emptied the sack straight into the pot.

Splash! Splash! Splash! In went the three heavy rocks and out came the boiling hot

water, all over the fierce young Fox and his
bad old mother. Oh, how sore and burned
and angry they were!

Never again did those wicked foxes
trouble the Cock, the Mouse and the Little
Red Hen, who always kept their door
locked, and lived happily ever after.

# The Little Porridge Pot

There was once a little girl who lived in a
village with her mother. They were very
poor and things got worse and worse until
one day they found that there was nothing
left to eat.

"I'll go into the forest and see if I can find
some berries," the little girl said. And off
she went.

She had not gone far when she met a
very old woman who smiled at her. "I
know that you are a good little girl and that
you and your mother are poor and hungry.

Here is a little pot to take home. Whenever you say to it, 'Cook, little pot,' it will fill itself full of delicious steaming porridge. When you have had all you can eat, you must say 'Enough, little pot,' and it will stop making porridge."

The little girl thanked the kind old woman and took the pot home to her mother. They were both so hungry that they could scarcely wait to say, "Cook, little pot."

At once the pot was full of porridge. Then, when they had eaten all they could, the little girl said, "Enough, little pot," and it was empty again.

From that day on, the little girl and her mother were never hungry any more, and they lived very happily for a while.

But one day when the little girl was out her mother wanted some of that delicious porridge all for herself. Carefully, she got the pot down from the shelf and said the magic words, "Cook, little pot." In a moment the pot was full.

The little girl's mother ate as much as she wanted. Then, suddenly, she screamed.

"Oh dear! Oh dear! I can't remember how to make it stop!"

The porridge kept on coming and coming. It filled the little pot to the brim. It seeped over the top and down onto the table. Bubbling and steaming, it overflowed onto the floor. More and more kept coming. The porridge ran across the floor and out of the door and streamed down the street. It went into neighbours' gardens! And into their houses! Finally, there was only one

house in the whole village that wasn't filled with porridge!

"Oh! Oh! Oh!" all the villagers cried at once. "Whatever shall we do?"

At that very moment, the little girl came home, and seeing porridge everywhere, she cried, "Enough, little pot."

To everyone's relief, the porridge stopped coming. However, they all had to squeeze into the one house that had escaped and live there together until, at last, they could eat their way back to their own homes.

# The Gingerbread Boy

There was once a woman who hadn't any children of her own and wanted one very much. One day she said to her husband, "I shall bake myself a nice gingerbread boy. That's what I shall do."

Her husband laughed at this idea but that very morning she mixed the dough and rolled it. Then she cut out a little boy shape with a smiling mouth and two currants for eyes. When she had popped him into the oven, she waited for him to bake and then she opened the door. Out jumped the gingerbread boy and ran away through the kitchen and right outside.

"Husband, husband," called the woman as she ran after the gingerbread boy.

The man dropped his spade when he heard his wife call and came running from the field.

But when the gingerbread boy saw the woman and the man chasing him, he only laughed, running faster and faster and shouting:

*"Run, run, as fast as you can,*
*You can't catch me,*
*I'm the gingerbread man!"*

On he ran until he met a cow.

"Moo! Moo!" called the cow. "Stop! Stop! I want to eat you."

But the gingerbread boy only laughed and ran faster than ever, shouting, "I've run away from a woman and a man and now I'll run away from you!"

*"Run, run, as fast as you can,*
*You can't catch me,*
*I'm the gingerbread man!"*

The cow chased after him but she was too fat and couldn't catch him. He raced on until he came to a horse.

"Neigh! Neigh!" snorted the horse. "You look good to eat. Stop and let me gobble you up."

But the gingerbread boy only laughed and shouted, "I've run away from a woman, a man, and a cow, and now I'll run away from you!"

"Run, run, as fast as you can,
You can't catch me,
I'm the gingerbread man!"

The horse galloped after the gingerbread
boy but couldn't catch him. He raced on
faster and faster until he came to some
farmers in a field.

"Ho! Ho!" they cried. "Stop! Stop! and let
us have a bite."

But the gingerbread boy only laughed
and shouted, "I've run away from a
woman, a man, a cow, a horse, and now I'll
run away from you!"

"Run, run, as fast as you can,
You can't catch me,
I'm the gingerbread man!"

The men joined in the chase but no one
could catch the gingerbread boy. He raced
far ahead until he came to a river and had
to stop. There he met a fox who wanted
very much to eat him then and there, but he
was afraid the clever gingerbread boy

might escape.

So he said politely, "Do you want to cross the river?"

"Yes, please," said the gingerbread boy.

"Well, then, jump on my back and I'll swim across."

"Thank you," said the gingerbread boy; and he did just that.

When they were about halfway across, the fox said, "The water is deeper here. I think you'd better crawl up onto my neck."

"Thank you," said the gingerbread boy; and he did just that.

When they had gone three-quarters of the way across, the fox said, "You'd better climb up onto my head. You can't be very comfortable there."

"Thank you," said the gingerbread boy; and he did just that.

"We're nearly there now," said the fox a moment later. "I think you'll be safer if you get onto my nice long nose."

"Thank you," said the gingerbread boy. But no sooner had he climbed onto the fox's nose than the fox threw back his head and SNAP! went his big mouth.

The gingerbread boy was half gone.

Then the fox did it again, SNAP!

The gingerbread boy was three-quarters gone.

The fox was having a very good time, and he did it again. SNAP! The gingerbread boy was all gone.

And that was the end of the gingerbread boy who had been too clever for the woman, the man, the cow, the horse, and the farmers. But not clever enough for the fox.